FISHTAILING

Wendy Phillips

COTEAU BOOKS

www.coteaubooks.com

Edited by Alison Acheson
Cover and book design by
Michel Vrána, blackeye.com

Printed and bound in Canada by
Friesens

The publisher gratefully acknowledges the financial support of its publishing program by: the Saskatchewan Arts Board, the Canada Council for the Arts, the Government of Canada through the Canada Book Fund, the Association for the Export of Canadian Books and the City of Regina Arts Commission.

Library and Archives Canada
Cataloguing in Publication

Phillips, Wendy, 1959–
Fishtailing / Wendy Phillips.
Poems.

ISBN 978-1-55050-411-8

1. Teenagers—Poetry. 2. Violence in adolescence—Poetry.
I. Title.

PS8631.H57F58 2009
jC811'.6   C2009-903993-1

10 9 8 7 6 5 4 3

COTEAU
BOOKS
FOR TEENS

2517 Victoria Avenue
Regina, Saskatchewan
Canada S4P 0T2
www.coteaubooks.com

Available in Canada from:
Publishers Group Canada
9050 Shaughnessy Street
Vancouver, British Columbia
Canada V6P 6E5

Available in the US from:
Orca Book Publishers
www.orcabook.com
1-800-210-5277

To Alison Acheson, for her sharp eye and encouraging voice

To Ted, for always believing in me

To James and Lucy, for reminding me how being young really feels.

To my students, whose writing keeps me alive to new ways of seeing.

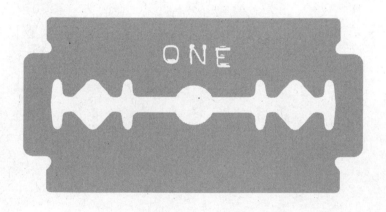

Tricia

Her glance
across the crowded classroom
speaks louder
than the droning recital
of paragraph structure.
I know you
    it says
You are mine
Something inside
shifts.

Miguel

In dreams
I swim through
underwater hallways
slapping my head
against the lockers
fighting the current
down the staircase
fishtailing forward.

They watch me
school eyes
do not blink
my scales shine
sleek
slippery.

I awake
mouth
open
fins
morphing
into fingers

to: Margaret Farr
from: Janice Nishi
subject: Natalie Anderson

Natalie Anderson (student number 062372)
has been enrolled in your English class.
She comes to us from a district secondary
school where she had some difficulty
with peer relationships. Please make her
welcome and keep me informed of any
difficulties.

Natalie

First day
at the new school
I can tell
it will be
like shooting
fish in a barrel.

Birthday

They're wrapped up here
in neat packages
bow on top
a little girl's birthday present.
I'm crashing this party
like always
A mark on my forehead
warns parents off
but draws innocents
like kids
to a clown.
Behind my makeup
a long-fanged
hook-clawed
monster.

by Natalie

Mrs. Farr

You have an admirable grasp of syntax
and a rich vocabulary. However, your images
are disturbingly violent. Perhaps you can
find more optimistic diction to flavour your
poetry. We can all use optimism.

Tricia

I know
my mother loved my father
once
wore a kimono
to please his family
learned to say *arrigato* and *sayonara*.
Jason is a carefully
friendly
stepfather

but where am I in this?
The mirror
shows my mother's round eyes,
my father's black straight hair.

I wonder
why she couldn't choose
someone
a little less
white.

Kyle

She doesn't know
I'm here.
Her hair
from the back
is like
black velvet
shiny
soft
my hand wants to stroke it.
My fingernails
are stained with grease.
I keep them tapping
my desk.

Miguel

Voices here
in fast English
talk of things
I don't know.

I know
the burn of hot sun
and blue water
the length of my father's back
in the bow
the thud of a soccer ball in the dust
the hum of my village at night.

My hands know
how to
paddle against an incoming tide
gut a fish

assemble
and shoot
a mobile
rocket launcher.

Natalie

Mum sold another house today.
She's passed out
on the couch
wine glass cradled
in her elbow.

Macaroni for supper again.
extra cheese
throw it all up later.

Mum's snores
float down the hall
to the TV room.

Jay Leno kisses me goodnight.

Miguel

In biology class
we do "dissection."
The other kids watch
as I cut open the perch
pin back its skin
on the wax tray
lay bare
its vital organs.

Kyle

My lab partner
may not talk much
but his fingers
know one end of the scalpel
from the other.

Tricia

Standing beside her
in the caf lineup
my flowered sweater wilts.
Her slouch just so
black-lined eyes
leather over belly ring
—something lithe in the line of her elbow—
in her hands
fries and gravy.
I look at my veggie wedges.
She cocks an eyebrow,
leans, shrugs.
Easy come, easy go.

Kyle

In Social Studies class
we do a skit on Canadian immigration
Sarah Yang, Kathy Lee, Miguel and me.
The girls make Miguel the star
because his accent is real.
I'm the bully who learns
his lesson.
Sarah and Kathy are peacemakers.

At the end
of course
we all belong.

Miguel smiles
at the applause.

Natalie

In English
it's silent
writing time.

Dust motes dance
on the earphones of the quiet
guy tapping his fingers

shine a halo
around the dark hair
clenched jaw
of the guy behind him.

He looks back.

His eyelids
close
and open

close again.

Feelings poem

Black, black, black
is the colour of my true love's hair.
Her lips are something roses fair,
The purest eyes and the neatest hands.
I love the ground on where she stands.

I love my love and well she knows.
I love the grass on where she goes.
If she on earth no more I see
My life will quickly fade away.

Black is the colour
Of my true love's hair.

Kyle

Mrs. Farr

I am glad to see you are reading poetry,
young man. However, "Black is the Colour" is
a traditional Scottish folk song. Presenting it
as your own constitutes plagiarism.

Please rewrite and see me.

Kyle

September sun
draws us to the soccer field.
Miguel leans against the fence
until I invite him in.
His footwork is beautiful.
He slips like a ghost
between defenders
sends it into the top corner.

As we head to the change room
we bump shoulders.
Our sweat dries in the cool afternoon.

Miguel

The new girl has a look
that cuts right
through the scales
to my cold fish heart.
I read Pablo Neruda
in bed
Spanish on one page
English translation beside it.

Into the night of the heart
your name drops slowly
and moves in silence and falls
and breaks and spreads its water. *

Nata Natalie Natalia
Sounds like music

* from "Slow Lament" by Pablo Neruda, trans.
Donald D. Walsh

Kyle

Nights at my dad's garage
I tinker with a timing chain.
You got good hands, kid,
my dad says.

The car is for Tricia's stepdad.
When he drops her at school
she waves him away
blows kisses at her little sister
in the back seat.

I tighten the bolts,
take extra care
to make it purr.

Tricia

School-issue gym shorts
sit cocky on her hips,
not bunched in T-shirt lumps
like mine.

Her slim legs flash
when she walks
the hem brushes a ring of cuts
around her golden thighs

I ask
she hits me with her lightning eye.
Cat, she says.

Running gym laps
we keep pace.
The other girls watch
from a distance.
I am chosen.

Miguel

On the soccer field
the air is full of joy
my feet remember the magic
and I forget everything else

until later.

Feelings poem – rewrite

A regular guy lived in Vancouver city
He liked a girl. She was pretty.
He thought to kiss her would be real fine.
He wrote her a poem. It's bad. It's mine.

by Kyle

Kyle

That black-haired poem
is what I mean,
not this nursery rhyme
crap.

My motorcycle fits together
neat and smooth
bolts and casings
pistons and pushrods
everything in place.

Words just lie
on the page
no schematics,
no fuel lines
no chassis.

A poem is a bucket
of bolts.

Feelings Poem

When the guns stopped
and the aid worker
pulled him out
from under the bed,
all was quiet
except his breathing
because he could not
hold it inside.

Vamenos, she said
and covered his eyes
but from under her fingers
he could see a leg
blood
his mother's kerchief.
In the street
flesh stuck to the walls
broken heads lay
in sticky red puddles
their bodies swollen, twisted,
full of bleeding holes.
Shhh, she said. *Tú eres seguro*
You're safe.

From Canada
it felt like a dream
or a poem
about feeling
afraid.

by Miguel

Mrs. Farr

Your narrative line of the Central American
village massacre rings with authenticity
and verisimilitude. It is a dreadful chapter
in that region's history, and an individual
tragedy for anyone involved in it. If this is
your experience, my sympathies.

In your poem, however, you dwell on blood
and carnage excessively. Perhaps an uplifting
moment of redemption is in order for the
protagonist. You might also reconsider your
point of view.

to: Janice Nishi
from: Margaret Farr
subject: Miguel

I am concerned about the violence in Miguel's poetry. Is there something I should know about behavioural anomalies that might affect the class's safety (or my own)?

to: Margaret Farr
from: Janice Nishi
subject: Re (1): Miguel

Miguel's traumatic experience has manifested itself only in withdrawal and periods of selective mutism. I do check on him regularly. There is no suggestion he poses a risk to anyone but himself.

Please keep me informed of any further concerns.

Tricia

Black heavy boots
heat up my feet.
Tight ripped T-shirt
digs into my armpits.
Natalie says
I'll get used to it.

Natalie

A scar cuts across his dark hand,
clenched on the desk,
a light flickers in his still brown eyes.
From the shift in his posture when I enter the
      room
the shake of his floppy hair
I know a tug on the line.
He's been caught before
and will require careful playing.

Tonight I prepare bait
hunch on the edge of the bathtub
paint toenails with glitter
shave calves silky
with the razor blade
make careful, measured slices
around my thigh
high enough
to hide under gym shorts
deep enough
to let the hurt out

I stroke the tender blue
skin of my wrist.
In my last school,
others told me,
across is for help

down is for goodbye.

From the mirror
she watches me
eyes narrowed.
Not today, she says.
Too many fish in the sea.

Ms. Nishi

My heels click
in the empty hallway
Lesson fragments flicker
from hushed classrooms
     a flash of a welding torch
      "the aqueous humour provides volume and
               shape…"
      "Your Fathers of Confederation hockey cards
               are due…"
      the heartbeat of a class set of jembe drums
I find Miguel in History.
When I pull him out his eyes dart
from lockers to water fountain
to hand-lettered posters.
Just checking, I assure him,
how you're managing.
His eyes at first dark
wild
then he slouches against the lockers
in a white-toothed grin.
Si, he says, *I'm fine*.
But for a moment I glimpsed
chaos.

Kyle

Last week
my fingers burned
to stroke
the length
of her smooth hair.
It pulled me
like a magnetic charge.
Now
it's clipped short
like feathers
and
my fingers still burn.

In the library
I watch her,
memorize the angle of
golden cheekbone
see
her mum's English eyes
her dad's Japanese skin
the best
of both worlds.

Her eyes skim over me
like tires over pavement
make me hum.

Tricia

The librarian tells us
we're here to distill
the truth
from its many representations.
I open the encyclopedia
to *Riel, Louis*

glaze over.

It's not that I don't love Emily.
My little half-sister
is two, curly, cute,
and she's all theirs.

but they hardly even noticed
when I cut my hair.

At the next table
Kyle opens
and closes
his hands
looks up from his book.

I can tell
he noticed.

Natalie

Sleep
escapes me.
I push aside my hot pillow
rise to my cold feet.

In front of the gas fire I smoke,
watch logs that never burn.

The flames curl like his hair.
Today I slipped my number into his pocket.
He didn't call.

I need to draw him out
or he'll snap
when I'm not expecting it.

When my eyelids finally close
I can still see the flames.

Kyle

Her hands
generate electricity.
When she takes one paper
passes the rest back
there's a spark.

Tricia

I've put her on
like new clothes
dark
edgy

Gone
the tremors
at a teacher's glare

the sickness in the pit
of my stomach
at Mum's disappointments

the storm in my brain
from rusty Japanese
after a weekend with my dad
and grandmother.

I meet the eyes
of guys who seek mine

eat french fries for lunch
chocolate milkshakes when I come home
easy come, easy go.

When Mrs. Farr asks
what the new image is about

I shrug, play with my tongue stud

Whatever.

No matter how hard she looks
she can't see me anymore.

Miguel

My mother swims
through the river of my dreams
nudges me gently
out of the shallows
floats downstream

belly up

Tricia

My mother
says Natalie
is a bad influence.
She phoned the school counsellor
asked her to move Natalie
to another class.

As if.
Natalie's spark
keeps me alive.

Homework is a constant mutter
class is a drone
except for the short, sharp
bite of the bell.

Kyle

In the mirror
I make five test runs.
Then I ask her
to help.

You do homework?
she says, a laugh
shakes her shoulders
like a choked engine.

Her dark eyes
on high beam.
Write a poem
about your motorcycle.
Farr would like that
she says.

I lean against the lockers
wheels spinning.

Miguel

Her number in my pocket
balled up
like a candy wrapper

It rolls between my fingers
promises
something sweet.

Mrs. Farr

I am becoming increasingly concerned, Tricia, about your growing list of assignments NHI.* However, I am sure you can complete them all before MCO** should you put your mind to it. I am available for consultation should you have any questions about EC***.

*not handed in
**marks cut off
***evaluation criteria

Tricia

The only other time
I was in the counsellor's office
was for career planning.

The future looks bright,
Ms. Nishi told me
then.

It's crowded now
me in one chair
in the other
my mother
stroking the baby hair
of my sister on her lap.
You've always been such a good girl.
she tells me.
Is this rebellion because of Emily?
You know Jason and I love you both.

I shrug.

Ms. Nishi moves
the desktop Zen garden.
A fluorescent bulb is blown
there are new shadows.

Assignment: Grammar poem
My motorcycle dream

(noun phrase)   The wind blowing in my face

(subordinate clause)   when I'm on my wheels

(verb phrase)   makes me fly

(simile)   like a bird on fire.

effect (2 lines)   I gun my engine till it roars
The pistons explode between my legs

(allusion)   I hear Bruce Springsteen
in my helmet screaming

(direct quotation)   "I'm chrome-wheeled fuel-injected
and steppin' out over the line."*

(conclusion)   I'm spinning down the streets
of my own runaway dream.

by Kyle

* from "Born to Run" by Bruce Springsteen

Mrs. Farr

A most effective (and might I say,
unexpected) example of a grammar poem.
You have made an excellent choice in writing
about a topic you care about so passionately.
However, you need to be careful of innuendo.
You might tone down the more overt sexual
references in order to make it suitable for
the poetry display board.

Kyle

sexual
references

?

Miguel

My uncle's jaw clenches
as he stands at the stove
holding the cooking spoon
with his two remaining fingers.

Tricia

Thanksgiving weekend
with my father
and Obasan.
I mumble through breakfast rice.
Dad hovers wistfully.

Out the window
gold leaves blanket
the repaired fishing nets
on rollers in the driveway

I think about Natalie
and me
laughing uncontrollably
making up our own language
to talk about boys.

I am
out of place
here.

Natalie

I am in the bath when the phone rings
I know it's him before he speaks
He hears me splash.

We're going to the Aquarium Saturday
lunch in the park.

I smile
as I push
END.

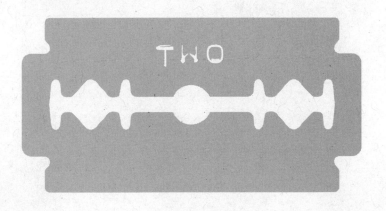
TWO

Kyle

West Coast rain
makes November
dark.
Bike tires
skid around corners
like my gut
when I pass her in the hall.
Cargo pants
sleeveless net shirt
eyes lined with black -
commando.
Sparks fly
from her eyes
settle on my bare skin
burn like fresh shrapnel.

Makeup assignment – social commentary poem

"Out of Step"

A soldier
steps out of line
on the road
from infantry
to adultery

drill sergeant yells
lieutenant halts the platoon
colonel writes a report
general reconsiders
the military objective.

She is swarmed
It's a jungle out there.
The company moves together.
Orders come from above.
Yours not to reason why
yours but to do
or die

the soldier looks back
sees the line
from a whole new perspective
marches

to her own
new
drummer

and the other war begins.

by tricia yamashita

Mrs. Farr
(makeup assignment: Tricia Y.)

An interesting analogy for teen rebellion, and you have foiled our expectations by making the soldier female.

However, I am concerned that you seem to regard adolescence as a war against authority. Superior officers often see the big picture. An army couldn't function if every soldier gave his own orders, now, could it?

Natalie

Mum's got a date
with Mr. TopSelling Remax
(local office).

She borrows my black sweater.
I feel just like a girl,
she twitters.
Don't wait up, Nat.

I try to write a poem for English.
drip frozen lasagne
not quite heated
on the keyboard
think about my father.

Mum says he's a monster
never gave her money
or compliments
or took her on dates
or watched me so she could go out.

She has no idea.
That's not a monster.

Miguel

The aquarium draws
me, slapping
waves, the squealing
breath of the sea lions, the blue silence
through the underwater viewing window.

The light on her face
leaves shadows
under her eyes
in the hollows of her cheeks
in the blue mask of her face
the eyes, so alive
dark lips smiling
faintly.

Social Commentary Poem

Internet Safety Workshop

Childhood is a bubble
    they tell parents
once burst, forever gone.

The burn on the retina of images that
should not be there
the screaming mouth of a
six-year-old victim

the luring come-on emails of the polished and
        hungry
saliva dripping from his mouth
as he pounds the keyboard,
licks his lips
squirms, turned on, before the web cam shots
of eager technokids

while blithe innocents google away
their afternoons
with a slide into darkness
frozen forever in the nowhere
that never disappears.

by Natalie

Mrs. Farr

This is a shocking poem, with a horrific message. You use impressive diction, Natalie, creating vivid images.

However, your response to our Internet Safety presentation does not follow the designated criteria. You show an almost voyeuristic depiction of detail of sexual predators and a hopelessness inherent in the innocence of children. The assignment required a solution to the problem. The nihilism in your poetry disturbs me.

Natalie

Solutions

disturb me.

Kyle

librarian says
songs count
gives me a library book
of '80s rockers
These are pretty hip,
she says.
I blow off the dust with laughing
find my dad's shower songs
my mum's red wine Friday dancing music.
Reading the lines
I feel the vibration of the speakers
through my sock feet
see my parents' arms
around each other.

Put some engine noise
to the words
they're not half bad.

I download them
to my iPod.

Tricia

Miguel's story was strictly
confidential
and whipped
through the school
like fire.
His scars impress us
parents lost
eyes haunted
almost wordless the first weeks.
We're gentle with him

Natalie's new.
When I told her, she promised
she wouldn't bite.

Natalie

At lunch we sit
together
she watches me slant-eyed.
I hear her voice
low
bored
cool
an edge I knew would sharpen
that first day.

I tell her about
the park
the dark viewing room
at the aquarium

She grins
Catch, she says
tosses the salt.

Miguel

I carry the blue glow
all weekend.

Monday morning
across the cafeteria
her look
remembers lips touching
hearts racing.
Her friend
watches
laughs

but I don't
look away

Kyle

Teacher staples my motorcycle dream
to the display board
Tricia wanders over
reads it
I watch
She turns
stares
raises an eyebrow
drifts to my table
Told you Farr would like it she says
Not bad.

I swallow a lump
Wanna ride sometime?
She lifts her chin
narrows her eyes
I look away from the glare
Yeah she says, *today*
walks away.

So
poems are good
for something.

Miguel

She comes up behind me
drapes herself over my back
nuzzles the nape of my neck

I leap clear
but I'm reeled in
by the hurt in her eyes

I thought you'd like that
    she says
I flounder for a second
Yes, I say. *I was only surprised.*

But it is hard for me.

Last time I cared
it ended
in explosions
blood
the end of everything.

Natalie

Miguel prefers shadows
But I tease him with exposure
I like the alarm in his eyes
when I hook a finger in his gills

Tricia

In Phys. Ed. we do warm-ups
Breathe deep, bend low, deep lunges, now.
and memory kicks in.

With every breath
the leather of his jacket
air thick with rain and cedar.
I press against his denim thighs
the solid muscle of his back
feel the surge of the bike.
Across the Starbucks table
brown hair flopped over his forehead
fingers laced around his coffee mug
rough fingers, black around the nails,
wonder how they'd feel across my cheek.
From the look in his eyes
he wonders too.

Right — six laps of the gym! Go!
My shorts sit cocky today.
Natalie and I run
step for step.

Natalie

Motorcycle boy
might be hot

but she'll have to learn
not to leave her friends behind.

Kyle

She fits on my bike
like a casing on an engine
like a fender on a wheel
like a nut on a bolt
When I gun the engine
it seems
it can roar
till next week.
Her arms around me
tighten around corners.
She laughs
breathes magic down
my neck.

Daydreaming in English
I flip through old poems
find it's not just me.
The light that blooms in your body
blooms in my hands. Around us the ground
is strewn with its petals. *

Suddenly
I can hear
poem voices.

* from "Poem without voices" by Robert Bringhurst

Miguel

At school
the Multicultural Leadership Committee
leave no one out.
They sell bashes at a piñata
for the trip to the Guatemala orphanage
fill the display case with a huge menorah.
Posters advertise the Diwali fashion show and
        fireworks display
respect the hungry Muslims for their Ramadan
        fast
invite canned food donations for Santa's
        breakfast.
The voices all shout at once.
The others attend all the parties.

But at home
it is not a party.
We are a household of men.
My cousin, my uncle, me,
all that's left.
We don't talk much.

Tenemos muchos diablos para quemar,
my uncle says, his words scorching.
We have many devils to burn.

We follow our new year tradition,
scour the house for anything *frivolo*
to throw away.

There is not much.

Kyle

We find corners
I'd never noticed

lean into them

breathe wordless
in each other's mouths.

We walk aimless
in the early dark.
Rain sizzles
on our faces.

Tricia

The rest of the country gripped
by a cold I cannot imagine.
My life has been lived in rain
according to coolly followed plans.

On TV the news reporter's breath puffs.
Between her flushed cheeks
and the camera
small hard snowflakes.

Miguel

Back home in the hot sun
school was outside
when the village was safe
before the teacher disappeared.

Here in Canada
the rain falls
day after day
and we keep everything
inside.

Kyle

The rain slides down
classroom windows
and my pen slides across the page.
Mrs. Farr's inbox yawns
like a monster rising from the deep
snapping at my ass
and words spill out.

As I write
the sun comes out
through raindrops.
A thousand colours scatter
across my page.

Tricia

Mum phones Aunt Susan back east
brags about the weather
Jason mowing the lawn in November
trips to the park with Emily's preschool crowd.
She'll send baby pictures of Em,
who's changing so fast.
Tricia? She's the same.

We love winters here, she says,
and we're all so happy,
so happy.

It's all shit.
Clouds leave a constant slanting drip
across the dull window.

I shake my head to dry my hair
think of Natalie's electric aura
our late nights
and of Kyle's leather shoulders .

I let it burn.

Kyle

Late at night
I strum my guitar
garage door closed.
The chords stroke the words
I write about her.

My voice
is changing.

Tricia

I tell Natalie
about skipping Chemistry
riding with Kyle
down the rain slick streets
our alcove encounters.
My heart pounds.
Bikes are a turn-on she laughs,
that smell of leather.
I smirk stupidly
with relief.

She rolls her eyes. *You could try mi novio.*
I'll try motorcycle boy.

I hold it back
but it shows.
Your eyes went weird she says
You gotta problem
sharing with friends?

We lock eyes.

No, I say, *yeah,*
I don't think
I want to.

She leans over

hugs me
whispers
Okay, okay.

Her perfume
intoxicates me.

Natalie

My sleeves are long
enough to hide
the lines carved
into the inner elbow.

I invite her in
With the jolt
we'll be fused
for good.

Miguel

Under her fingers
slowly
my arms open
draw her inside
the circle, hold her
against me.

Our lips
our eyelids
are slow
soft.

Tricia

She promises
a river of forgetting
a sensation
past imagining.
My heart
trembles
before her eyes
and I see myself
new.

Natalie

I'll say this.
His hands know
how to heat up
my blood.

Winter solstice celebration poem assignment

At the *loas* the virgin
looks the devil in the eye
He breathes fire on her
dances, tells her,
You'll lose.
He turns to the audience
and for a minute,
the Central American Community Centre
with echoing stage, silk plants, old curtains
becomes the bright
hot afternoon in the village square
the Virgin of Guadeloupe standing tall
driving down with her will
this quivering devil.
Villagers' houses
are empty of vanities.
They shout *No*! and the devil melts
under her hot eyes.
The virgin wins.

The villagers explode fireworks
shoot off guns that were
hidden in boxes
under beds
in closets
against the ceasefire rules.

In the background a Canadian salsa band
calls through the microphone
that they will
take it away.

by Miguel

Mrs. Farr

Your celebration is not one with which I am
familiar. Interesting personal connection
with the local centre and the description of (I
assume?) your own village square. You seem
to find writing cathartic and therapeutic.

Curious how many solstice celebrations
involve cleansing rituals, setting the world
to rights before beginning afresh. Wouldn't
we all like to have that chance? Those devils
don't always melt away, though, do they?

Tricia

She frees me from
the good girl inside
brings those dim dissatisfactions
into focus
sharpens my edges.

I owe her.

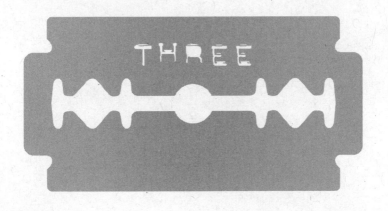

Natalie

Mum's gone again
conference weekend at Whistler
motivational seminars all morning
ski all afternoon
screw their brains out
when the fire dies down.
She frowns when I talk this way.

I call my father. Six thirty
and his tongue is already thick
words slurred
his random heartiness
booms and fades.

He says
You're okay, right hon.
(not a question.)
I say
Fine, Dad, fine. Great.
He says
I may make it to Vancouver
one of these days,
or you could take a bus
to the Interior. I could pick you up.
I say
I don't think so.

I don't think so.
I don't think so.
I don't think.
Don't think.

Kyle

Ms. Nishi
calls me in to the counselling office.
Tricia's mother
says someone is
leading her astray
wherever that is.
I give Ms. Nishi my poems.
She reads
looks at me sharp
flips the page to read the comments.
*You have a voice
of your own.*
I shrug
I like to ride my own road.
She reaches for a careers booklet
flips the pages
shows me a new world
of possibilities.

Ms. Nishi

They bleed all over the page
but she sees ink
nudges it into startling shape
with a red pen.

Natalie – Memory...1

New email new address
doesn't wipe out
my last paternal contact.
Dad, passed out in the La-Z-Boy
CD blaring
the Avril Lavigne I bought for him
that he never plays.

His upstairs neighbour, Andy
mouth lazy
arm languid
draped over the back of the couch
fingers hooked over my shoulder.

Pink lemonade gin courses
through my veins
blurs
the feeble shakes
of my head

Miguel

My cousin, Juan, says
tradition is a lie.

No one defeats the devil
And we are not
sick of sin.

*We may have left
but our people still need our help
and we will send it to them.*

Then he laughs.

*But it's not for you to know,
muchacho.*

Kyle

I almost don't need
to see her
She's welded on the inside
of my eyelids
her voice whispers
in the strings
of my guitar.

Miguel

Natalie's hands are soft
Her laugh is sharp
Her words cut.

At home
we do not talk.
We simmer.
I miss my parents
but do not speak of them.

When it won't stay inside
any longer
I punch the brick wall
in the alley.

My hands ache
my knuckles bleed
I can see what hurts.

Natalie – Memory...2

Wanna show you something, he tells me.
Dad's snoring. We leave him there.
His hand under my arms
He pulls me up the stairs.
My legs fold
my head spins.
The door lock clicks behind us.

His screen saver flips
from centerfold
to centerfold
heads flung back
lolling tongues
swollen breasts
gaping vaginas
That's only the beginning
he says,
plays a loop of iMovies
watching my face.
My stomach lurches
at the desperate
disconnected
eyes of the children

He switches on the webcam
pushes me back on the bed.
traps my wrists

in one hand.
My head rolls back
and forth on the blanket.
The voice
that wails
from my throat
is not mine.

to: Janice Nishi
from: Margaret Farr
subject: Natalie

I am concerned about Natalie's tendency to write on inappropriate topics. She attempts to draw attention to herself by including shocking, violent, nihilistic details. Perhaps you can speak to her about exercising some restraint.

to: Margaret Farr
from: Janice Nishi
subject: Natalie

Natalie has a disturbed home life, and I believe the school district has not been told the whole truth about her past. I don't believe she has learned much about restraint. I will have a word with her.

Natalie – Memory...3

Dad's still asleep
when I stumble downstairs
my stomach churning
my body bruised
and burning.

It smells of smoke
and old couches.

I crawl
oozing
into bed.

When I get home
Andy sends me an email
tells me I'll be
famous.

I throw up.
Change my
address.
Start a work of art
in blood
on my thigh.

Tricia

She's taken me
into her confidence.
I have no cat
she says.

Her house is empty
She lives in delicious silence
Mum at work
No toys
or two year old
or mother in a sour milk
marshmallow bathrobe
or family pictures where
she doesn't match.

We eat Lean Cuisine meals
for afternoon snack.

Watch me, she says.
sits on the edge of the tub
razor poised like a paintbrush
over the blank canvas of her arm.
With each touch a tracery
of beaded bubbles
winking to the surface.

Now you.

We look at each other
like we're about to kiss.

Natalie

She holds the blade
like it will bite
slips as I knew she would
afraid to be afraid
gushes, spurts blood.
With a cry
she clamps a cloth to her arm
folds into her elbow.

I pull her open
Feel it, I say, *feel it.*

What? she says.
Her frightened eyes dart
like a bird in a cage

But the red drip drip drip
on the polished linoleum
is our bond.

Miguel

Beside my village
ran a blue river
where the canoes lay
on the sandy shore.

Juan tells me,
for a week
after that day,
it was so choked
with bodies
you could not breathe
for the smell.
My father's
was among them.

Juan says the blood
made the river run
red.

Ms. Nishi

Notes on Natalie Anderson 10:45 a.m. Nov. 20.
Pulled Natalie out of Math to discuss concerns
expressed by M. Farr. N says she vents her anger
with her parents (separated) through poetry. New
boyfriend (Miguel Ruiz) (positive influence)?
Scheduled counselling session Nov. 27, 11 a.m.

Tricia

I try to avoid Kyle
to protect him from Natalie.
His muscles are hard
but his eyes flicker
with need.
When our eyes catch
only the prickle of dried blood in my elbow
keeps my knees from buckling.
I pick at the scab.

Kyle

I see her cheek in the curve
of my guitar
her slim fingers
in the frets.
Power is in her fingertips.
I am driven.

Miguel

From soft whispers
her voice hardens
Tricia and I are best friends, she says.
We share everything.

Her eyes are open
but closed to me.
She can see out but I can't see in.

My mouth is open
but no air comes in.
I'm out of my element.

Ms. Nishi

A steady stream today
in the hallway outside
the counselling suite

Something
has awakened them
skin thinned
blood pulsing below the surface.

Poem about Poetry

My words
like gears
drive thoughts
through school traffic congestion

My voice
like an engine
roars along the passing lane
in internal combustion

My poem
like a loose fan belt
spins on its pulley
with a high-pitched scream

Put it to music
The world would listen then
as I am listening now.

by Kyle

Mrs. Farr

Engine similes are powerful, Kyle (no pun
intended.) I notice you have copied the
structural pattern of Shelley's "To a Skylark,"
an unexpected but notable allusion.

to: Janice Nishi
from: Margaret Farr
subject: Kyle

I am concerned about Kyle's sudden
discovery of poetic aptitude. Having
caught him once in an act of plagiarism
I am concerned he is being dishonest
again. Perhaps you can speak to him about
intellectual integrity. Goodness knows I've
made few inroads.

Kyle

from smoulder to flame
and back again
Tricia's eyes flicker
towards Natalie
as I approach
then
dismiss me.

Miguel

At night
I smear ointment on my bleeding knuckles.
Uncle Eduardo,
deep in phone conversation,
does not notice minor injuries.
He plans to drive out the devils
find freedom through the barrel of a gun
make our home a shrine to justice.

The government troops are moving again,
Juan whispers. *Our people are defenceless.*
He smiles.
But not for long.

I go back to bed
pull the covers over my head,
dream of dodging gunfire
as I float down a blood river
on a raft of human bones.

Tricia

They're a lovely family
I'm sure.
Mom and Jason dress up
for the preschool parents' potluck
Emily looks adorable in frilled overalls
and big blue eyes.

I so don't belong here.

Kyle

In the garage, door closed,
I bring out my guitar
play till it hurts
same chords over and over
till I don't have to think
the voice in my head screaming
till it's all I can hear.

Thoughts on razor blades

The smooth surface of school
invites perforation
penetration
The teachers wear polite masks
that look in only one
direction.
Such a blank canvas begs
the artistry of the razor,
the bloody beauty
of wounds.

by Natalie

Mrs. Farr

I'm afraid I cannot give balanced praise and criticism to this hardly veiled threat. I am forced to submit a copy of your assignment to the administration for disciplinary measures.

Ms. Nishi

The poem lies before me,
decorated with Post-It forms
from teacher and admin.
The counsellor form is still blank.

Her blank gaze confronts me
across the desk
She rakes the mini Zen garden,
separates all the rocks
digs a moat around each
with her little finger.

Really, she says, there's nothing more
I want to tell you.

Miguel

In the midnight playground
I meet Natalie
We hold hands in side-by-side swings
slide off to hold each other
in the gravel.

She kisses my mouth open
with watermelon lips
Her hands fumble inside my shirt
stroke down to my jeans
Are you hungry for me?
she whispers into my mouth.

I am lost in her breath.
Yes, I tell her.
Yes, yes.
I am wide open.

A dog walker's flashlight
breaks us apart
gasping.

Dear Mr. and Mrs. Lawson

Kyle's Tech teacher has suggested Kyle consider
a career in mechanics, as he has a natural talent
in this area. He wants to take Kyle to the Trades
Career Fair on the Professional Day next week.
If you agree, please sign the attached waiver and
permission form and return to me by Friday.

Sincerely

Ms. J. Nishi
Counsellor
Career Advisor

Kyle

My dad says
he wants to frame the note.
The first step down your father's road!
He spreads his hands on the kitchen table
strong fingers, nicked with healing scratches.

My hands clench.
Voices sing in my head.
I used to be so certain.

My mum smiles.
Just keep your options open.

Mrs. Farr

The ProD day seminar
is on the Adolescent Battle for Emotional
Development
and the Role of the Teacher in the Trenches.
The presenter
livewired with a remote control
computer projections
complete with iMovie case studies,
tells me I am the front line
that it's my job
to measure negative self image
uncover the disturbing secrets
of my 218 students,
then save them from themselves.

I'm sorry.
After twenty-six years of adolescent crises
it takes a lot to move me.
I can teach them to write.
End of story.

Miguel

I get home late
Uncle Eduardo is in the spare room
kneeling before an open wooden crate.
Inside guns nest in wood shavings.

He watches Juan
lift one out
stroke the curls of wood from the blue barrel
reach forward with the sight
tip the door shut
in my face.

Tricia

Natalie tells me exactly
how far to go
how to pull back
leave him wanting.

I tell her I will.
I don't tell her
I want him too.

Miguel

She ignored me today,
slapped my hand away.
I lie awake in darkness
hear my uncle's voice
on the midnight telephone.

Uncle Eduardo tells me nothing.
I promised your mother,
he says
but Juan gives clues.
A truck will head south next week.
Until then, they are ours to protect.

My mother's ghost hand reaches out
of the water
to stroke my face.
Why does it hurt so much? I ask.
There is more to love than pain, she whispers.
Her face ripples
is gone.

Maybe
but I cannot see it.

Natalie

Bring him along
then cut him cold
leaves him with an unquenchable thirst.
Poor boy.

Kyle

The hum of a well-adjusted motor
filters into my secret guitar harmony.
A stash of music
locked in my tool box.
I take it out
when no one's around
my worker fingers
pluck from the strings
a delicate disharmony.

Mum looks in sometimes,
shuts the door behind her.
She knows
but no one else does.

Tricia

In the girls' change room
he freezes.
I pull him into a shower stall
and in a minute we're kissing
and I can't breathe
something inside me is exploding
and I don't want to stop

but as agreed
Natalie sends in the Phys. Ed. teacher
who pulls aside the curtain
glowers.

Kyle

In the garage
I sing for her, my voice
raspy and raw.
From the look in her eyes I think
I've crossed over.

Miguel

Today she let me hold her hand
touched me with feather fingers
smiled deep in my eyes.

She still wants me.

Kyle

In a rare
sunny lunch hour
we take the soccer ball
out to the wet field.

We're soaked with mud
and sweat.
Miguel's bandaids peel off.
His knuckles are raw.
Hey man, I ask him.
Fell, he answers.

Natalie

Mum's moving
to the next stage
in her relationship,
a weekend at the hot springs,
just the two of them.

Whatever

I wouldn't
have wanted to come anyway,
and besides
it must be
party time.

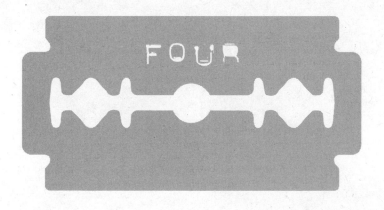

Tricia

You going to Natalie's Friday? Kyle asks me.
He's wary.
I don't talk to him at school.
I look around. *Yeah. You?*
He rakes me with a look that leaves me
weak-kneed.
I squeeze my thumb into my elbow.
See ya.

Kyle

In Ms. Nishi's office
we talk about
music futures
decisions
family dreams
and it slips out
about Miguel's hands.
Shit.
Hope she's cool.

Ms. Nishi

A flurry of pink phone messages
after the program planning sessions.
I'll need the Spanish teacher to translate
for the call to Miguel's uncle.
Another stall in the request
for confidential files.
Irate call from Kyle's father.

In the halls
I hear talk about
something coming.

Tricia

My mother lives
on another planet.

The sliding door from the family room
to the dark back yard
rumbles a little
in the midnight house
but not too much.

Miguel

My father never visits me
in dreams.
Uncle Eduardo tells me it is because
his spirit lives on
in our dreams of freedom.

But I read another voice

Hatred has grown scale on scale,
blow on blow, in the ghastly water of the swamp,
with a snout full of ooze and silence. *

I don't hear my father
because he is silent.

* from "The Dictators" by Pablo Neruda

Tricia

After school
I go to Natalie's to help
with preparations.
Her place is clean as a show house.

Washtub for ice
for beer and coolers
(Natalie has connections)
bowls for chips and dip
pick out music.

At midnight
we bring out the razor.
My touch is surer now
and as the blood wells to the surface
I can almost taste it.

At home I start my homework:
    immigration policies of the West essay
    cancer cell diagram
    quadratic equations.

The hush of the sleeping house
presses on my shoulders.

to: Janice Nishi
from: Margaret Farr
subject: Tricia

I am concerned about Tricia's decline in
English class. Her latest efforts have been
desultory and sporadic, and verging upon
disrespectful. Perhaps you can speak to her
about her lack of focus.

Tricia

My old friends
my mother
my teachers
warn me off Natalie.

But I see her more clearly.
Crossed red lines
mark us both
bind us with secrecy.

In the hall we link arms
blood and sparks
flow between us.

Kyle

At the grads' coffee house
I step up to the open mike.
My throat opens
in time to my drumming heart.
Heads swivel towards me.
In front, beside Natalie
Miguel nods in time.
At the back with the other
teacher chaperones
stands Mrs. Farr,
her eyebrows raised
in surprise.
But mostly I see Tricia
her eyes shining.
I sing to her.

Natalie

So he's not just
motorcycle boy.
That raspy voice belongs to
star maker machinery.
But there's more than one way
to get attention.

Tricia

His voice is raw
and his guitar vibrates
under his magic fingers.
Through it all
he looks at me, sings
about a knife
that cuts deep
and feels right.
He sees
inside me.

Kyle

When my dad asks
over dinner
how the career fair went
I tell him
I'm not going to trade school.
I wanna be a musician.

My father's back stiffens.
That's not a career, he says. *It's a hobby.*
And you won't see a penny from me.
(*Now dear*, says my mother)
Your old man's work isn't good enough for you,
is that it?

Dad, I say, *Dad*
you got it wrong.

But he waves my words away
like they're nothing.
I slam the garage door,
play the same chords
again and again.

Makeup assignment:
Poem about Poetry

Write a poem, the teacher says,
put in it your deepest feelings
so I can give you
carefully worded encouragement
constructive criticism
and a mark out of ten
to factor into the class average.

Here you go.

by tricia yamashita

Mrs. Farr

Your assignment borders on insolence. Please rewrite in a vein more suited to the spirit of the assignment.

Kyle

Since the coffee house
the kids turn and move aside,
whisper me a route
through crowded halls.

Tricia

With the Friday afternoon bell
we ride the wave of students
out the front door
sloughing off school
like an old towel.

In the crush
I feel a hand at my waist
breath in my ear.
I'll be looking for you
tonight
Kyle whispers
then catches the current
to the motorcycle parking.

Natalie grabs my elbow
Party time,
she says,
pulls me along.

Natalie

I turn up the music
feed Tricia strawberry coolers
In the kitchen
I sip rum and coke.
No more gin
for this girl.

Tricia

by 10:30
the voices are so loud
they drown out the music

Miguel

by midnight
it is difficult
to move through
the noise and bodies
I hear glass breaking
drunk laughter
things are coming apart.

Kyle

I have no party language
spot a guitar
strum a few chords
and around me clusters a circle
of wondering faces.
Beyond them
Tricia stares
catches my breath,
slips away.

Natalie

Loud strangers
crowd the house.
The spreading stains and destruction
feed my emptied stomach.

Tricia

Someone has broken
the fern.
Natalie pulls me behind it
slips me a note.
Timing is everything, she says.
I fight my way to the living room
to find Miguel.

Kyle

Natalie sidles down beside me.
She'll be waiting for you
when the song ends,
leaves a whispered kiss on my earlobe.
My fingers slip
on the fret.

Miguel

In the dark room
kids lean into one another's bodies
sway to the heartbeat of the music.

My father loved to dance
but when the soldiers came
his ears heard only the music
of the guns.

Tricia pushes through the shadows
towards me
The ghosts inside
are louder than music.

Kyle

The lights are off.
When I call her name she whispers
Shh
pulls me to the pillow
her hands move
quick
across my body
peel off my T-shirt
before snatching
my breath
with a hungry mouth
that tastes of watermelon
and I know
it's not Tricia.

Miguel

There is
heat
in my mind
party music cannot
cool.
Tricia hands
me a note:
up the stairs
2nd door on the right
I'm waiting. N.
I mount the stairs
two at a time
The hallway light
reveals
a bare torso.
Kyle's.
Miguel, she breathes,
and the heat
explodes.

Natalie

Miguel's face
an orgasm of anger
his body an explosion
of motion
as he lunges
towards the bed.

Tricia

I hear a roar through
a haze of coolers
and the thudding
bass
in the kitchen
speaker

panic
and Natalie's name

Up the stairs in slow
motion
and Miguel's fist
smashing into
a face
again
and again
the meaty thuds
in ridiculous
synchronization
with the party
music
and I see
he's killing
Kyle.

Natalie

When the others
drag Miguel away
push him
swearing and swinging
through the front door
Kyle's face
looks like raw meat
but he's breathing.
It was so passionate
it was poetry

Tricia

What is he doing here?
I left him playing to his audience.
From the bed
I hear
Natalie breathing
loudly.
Electricity snaps
through the air
between us.

I expected Miguel
and he…
her eyes shine with tears.

Kyle rises
on one elbow
his ruined face beseeching
I thought she was you.

I turn
to comfort Natalie.

Miguel

I stumble through empty streets
before my eyes float
Natalie's half smile
the laughing faces of soldiers
my father's limp body.
My fists smash the cement wall
jar pain
up to my shoulders
I hear a groan
that must be
me.

Tricia

When the police come
they say
The neighbours made
a noise complaint.
When Kyle staggers
bleeding
down the stairs
they say
Let's go, kid.

We're bathed in
flashing blue silence
at the doorway
and I realise
the music has stopped.

Miguel

Stupid boy, says my uncle,
to bring the police to this house.
You know what we have here.
The police are not our friends.

On a kitchen chair
in the corner
Juan smoulders

In my room
I stare at the ceiling.
My mother's voice is silent.

The room around me
narrows to a black tunnel
and in a blinding light of understanding
I see
I have no choice.

Tricia

As dawn breaks she tells me
it was her best performance poetry
Kyle's shock
Miguel's anger
my loyalty.
The house is shattered around her
and she's laughing so hard she's crying.
I back carefully
out the door.

Miguel

From under the bed
I pull a gym bag
slide out the blue barrel
stroke the trigger
cradle the gun in my bleeding hands

The cylinder
makes a clean click, click, click.
I pull back the hammer.

Natalie

Mum was so pissed
by the end of her weekend
she said next stop
was a foster home.
I told her she was lucky
she had connections
in the home repair business.

Ms. Nishi

To: All staff
Re: Weekend tragedy.

Many of you will have heard of the death of one of
our senior students, Miguel Ruiz.
He was a refugee from a war-ravaged region and
had been suffering from depression.
Please be sensitive to student grief and let students
know that crisis counselling will be made available
in this time of sorrow. Counselling is also available
to staff members.

Kyle

My face will heal
with adjustments
they tell me.
They don't know about the rest.

Tricia

Ms. Nishi says
it's not my fault
but I was the one
who turned away.
She says
I can turn back
but I'm afraid.

Then I remember
Miguel's the one
who can never turn back.

Ms. Nishi

When I tell her
Options Alternate School
is her last chance
Natalie shrugs.
Her mother looks at her watch.
She's beyond me, she says.

As they leave
I fix her with
unprofessional
anger.

She looks back
haunted.

Natalie

They look at me
like
I'm a monster.
Sometimes
in the mirror
in a moment of stillness
I see beneath my skin
hooked claws
fangs.

Sometimes
he still stirs
in blue shadows.

When I cry
I make sure
no one sees.

to: Janice Nishi
from: Margaret Farr
subject: grief

I appreciate your offer of grief counselling,
but I don't think I'll need emotional support.
I have my own coping methods.

Tricia

The pain
has nothing to do
with the breakfast
that sits still
in my stomach.

My footsteps make no echo
on these floors,
washed clean daily
of spilt blood.

At the nurse's station
they tell me
how to find him.

I'm sorry
I whisper
*I should have believed
you.*

His rough hand
on my arm
makes my blood
sing.

Kyle

At school I mutter
through clenched teeth
and jaw wire
my face a tire tread
of stitches

but
Tricia's fingers on my cheek
let me smile.
I tell her
kissing will be safer
without the tongue stud.

Ms. Nishi

After school
in the staff parking lot
Margaret Farr
hunches over the steering wheel
clutches an armload of papers

through the rainy window
I can see
she is crying

Tricia

After Miguel's memorial service
My shoulder nudges Kyle's arm
we walk so close.
Outside, under the oak tree,
I hug him so tight
he winces,
grins,
cries.

On the road
my face pressed against his jacket
the bike roaring between us

I smell spring.